SUNRISE OVER
FIRE ROCK FIELD

JOHN M. DOLBEY   MAE L. DOLBEY

**For my
wonderful
daughter, Mae.**

Your ongoing fascination and
love for dinosaurs inspired me to create
the Iggy adventure. This began as daily
storytelling in the car on our way to school and
has continued for more than four years. I
love you dearly and know that we
will both treasure this story
forever as I do
you.

Mae's illustration of Iggy.

CONTENTS

Far Forest
Fire Rock Field
Swim Lake
Herds United
Forest
Water Falls
Rocky Shore
Bath Lake
Lush Grazing Fields
Steep Canyon Walls

Volcano

Plant Eater's Field

Herd Practice

creek

Iggy's
Den

Forest

Grassy Hill

Council
of
Elders

Dawn, Iggy, and Guana (left to right)

CHAPTER 1
Dinner Time

Iggy carefully stepped through the dry and crunchy forest floor. He pointed his nose to the sky. Burning evergreen trees and bushes grew closer to his home and forest every day. The smoke made him cough and sneeze. He could not stop to worry about that.

Iggy closed his eyes and sniffed to his left and to his right. He galloped through the forest, straight ahead.

"I know you are out there somewhere!" Iggy yelled. "And you better not giggle!" he said even louder.

He stopped. Iggy heard the bouncy laugh of his two younger sisters. With a quick leap, he landed behind the large rock in front of him.

"I found you, Guana and Dawn! I win again," Iggy said.

"Iggy, that's not fair," yelled Dawn. "I'm the baby sister. You have to let Guana and me win sometime!"

"Next time, you two can look for me," Iggy said.

"Wait, stop," Guana whispered. "Do you hear that?"

Their mother's familiar voice called them through the trees. She interrupted their game. "Iggy, Guana, Dawn, time for dinner. Come home now."

The three iguanodons ran toward home. They didn't care about the path they made leaving their den. They crashed through the trees and bushes so they could get home faster. Small lizards and beetles jumped into their holes. Frogs hid behind large rocks to keep from getting trampled.

Iggy was in front. He cleared the way for his smaller sisters with his long and powerful front arms. Branches bent and broke ahead of them. As they got closer to home at the edge of the forest, the path widened. Iggy slowed down. Guana and Dawn passed him.

"Beat you!" Dawn yelled.

"You sure did," Iggy said with a smile.

Guana looked at Iggy. She knew Iggy let them win. She playfully pushed him into a small tree, and they both laughed and left the forest. The iguanodon siblings were growing up fast. Six-year-old Iggy was almost ten thousand pounds, nearly as big as a full-grown iguanodon.

Four-year-old Dawn and five-year-old Guana were still a lot smaller than Iggy. They had long snouts and powerful hind legs and tails. Strong front arms helped them to run fast and to protect themselves when in danger.

Iggy, Guana, and Dawn walked across the small creek that ran in between the forest and their den. Their mother and father waited for them on the other side.

Dawn

CHAPTER 2
Sad About Salad

"Iggy, Guana, Dawn, your food is here. I brought it from Plant-Eater's Field," their mother said.

"Not the same old salad!" Dawn exclaimed.

"Yeah, can't we have something different?" Guana asked.

The dinosaur siblings talked about the other food they used to eat before the Great Fire. Back and forth they talked, faster and faster, louder and louder.

Their father, Juras, swung his large head and scratched at the ground with his long thumb spike.

The young iguanodons stopped talking. Compared to most iguanodons, Iggy's dad had very long thumb spikes, and he could use them well.

"We are plant-eaters," Juras said impatiently. "We eat what we have. Tomorrow you can look for other food."

"We have looked, Father," Guana said sulking. "All of the best food burned up in the fire. It's not growing back!"

They all looked down glumly at their food. Boring salad just sat there.

"You must remember," their father said, "before the Great Fire, we had more places to look for food. The plant-eaters had more fields and more forest and more fresh water."

Dawn crinkled her nose and squinted her eyes. She had heard this before.

He continued, "We now have less food, and we have to share with all of the plant-eaters. But our field is the safest for plant-eaters now. What is the most important thing to remember?" he asked.

"We know," Iggy, Guana, and Dawn all said together in grumbly voices. "Stay away from where the meat-eaters live, especially Evil T-Rex and his family from Far Forest."

"That's right," Juras said sternly. "Those meat-eaters are all bad and mean. They would eat you for any meal or just for fun. And Evil T-Rex is the worst.

"You must trust me about this," he added. "I know. We are good, and they are bad. It is that simple. Now eat your food and thank your mother."

"Thank you, Mother," they all whispered.

"You are welcome, fine iguanodons," Iggy's mother, Maya, said.

"I still don't like this salad," Dawn said, too soft for anyone to hear.

They all gobbled up their greens. Dawn covered her last bite by pushing some dirt over it with her fingers.

Iggy remembered their meals before the Great Fire, which was almost two big moons ago. They had many kinds of berries, nuts, mushrooms, sweet honeycomb, and yes, greens. He closed his eyes and could almost taste the food. It was so good.

The fire still burned in some parts of the forest. Red firewater bubbled, oozed, and slowly snaked closer to Plant-Eater's Field every day. It came down from the top of the nearby mountain. The smoky smell was always in the air.

The sky turned darker. Iggy, Guana, and Dawn did not need their mom and dad to tell them it was time to go to sleep. Smoke left a haze in the sky, and it was hard to see the sun's rays. The heat of the day was still enough to warm the rocks in their den.

They huddled together in their favorite spot, against the large stone at the edge of the den. They would be comfortable together for a while. It was much cooler later at night.

Iggy thought to himself about what his father had said about the t-rex family. *Did they just growl, chase, and eat plant-eaters? Would they ever come to Plant-Eater's Field? Were they really as bad as his father was saying? Or did they talk together over dinner like Iggy and his family and wish for better times?*

Iggy slept restlessly that night. His mind was consumed with confusion and questions.

Tail Whip

CHAPTER 3
Herd Practice Begins

Fog and silence filled the morning air. Iggy woke up before his sisters and parents. He blinked his sleepy eyes.

His stomach flip-flopped, but Iggy was not hungry. Today was the final challenge at herd practice. He was very excited. Every year, the young iguanodons learned more and more about being in a herd. The larger iguanodons also learned how to protect and lead a herd.

"Dawn, Guana! Come on; let's go!" Iggy called out. "I can't be late today, and you have to be there, too."

Dawn and Guana wobbled to their feet and blinked at the morning light. Iggy bumped into them. He pushed them both out of the den towards the creek.

"You better run with me. You don't want me to win, do you?" Iggy teased. He ran along the creek. Guana and Dawn ran right behind him.

Iggy jumped into the creek and galloped straight through it. Water splashed everywhere. He ran so fast and was so excited that he didn't see the triceratops drinking from the creek up ahead. It stood in the shallow water on its thick legs. The sun shined off of its large, gray neck frill.

The three iguanodons thundered through the water and soaked the triceratops. Guana almost got a horn in her side. She was the last to pass the very upset three-horn.

They reached the far end of Plant-Eater's Field not a moment too soon. Iggy and his sisters joined the group of iguanodons and stayed quiet. Saber, their teacher, began to speak.

"Today is a big day," Saber said. "We find out which young iguanodons will be ready to help defend the herd. If you pass this challenge, you will join the adult iguanodon defenders and you may lead the herd one day. Let's get started."

Iggy's mother and father arrived along with the other parents. They watched from the edge of the forest.

All of the younger iguanodons gathered together to form a small herd, including Guana and Dawn. Iggy and the bigger iguanodon children stayed together and waited their turns.

Saber called out for the first iguanodon to take the lead. Tail Whip looked around. All of the other plant-eaters just looked back at him.

"I guess it's my turn," Tail Whip said with a crackly voice.

He stepped in front of the practice herd and held his head high. He was just happy that everyone watched him. Tail Whip was just a little younger than Iggy but was much smaller and less powerful. He did happen to have an unusually long, skinny, whiplike tail.

"Go get 'em!" Iggy yelled out.

The herd of smaller iguanodons followed Tail Whip. The forest crashed and boomed suddenly and loudly! Five large adult iguanodons galloped into the field, straight at the herd.

"Ahhh!" Tail Whip screamed.

He started flinging his long tail left and right. The herd scattered. Adults quickly knocked over the smaller iguanodons. Tail Whip's eyes closed tightly.

The adults stood over five young members of the practice herd. They snorted and kicked dirt and grass on them. Then the adults walked back into the forest.

"Not a good day for Tail Whip," Juras whispered to Maya off to the side.

With eyes still shut tight, Tail Whip tossed his tail side to side, trying to hit something. He succeeded only in blowing the grass and dirt around.

"Hey, Guana, you look pretty funny with dirt all over your face!" Iggy yelled from the side.

"I don't like this practice!" Guana screamed back. "I hate getting so dirty."

Dawn stood nearby. "You need to move faster, big sister! No one caught me that time," she said proudly.

"Okay, okay," Saber called out. "Good try, Tail Whip, but you still need more practice. And it might help to keep your eyes open."

Quiet snickers went through the practice field.

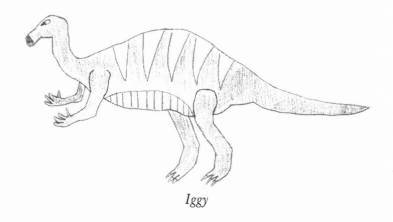

Iggy

CHAPTER 4
Iggy's Turn

The iguanodons prepared for more practice after a short rest. Dusty air settled to the ground. Iggy looked over at his father.

"Iggy, you're up next," Saber said.

Iggy's stomach still churned. He was the oldest iguanodon in herd practice and wanted to spend more time with the adults, protecting the herd. Iggy wanted to make a better life for his family. He stepped in front of the practice herd. Saber gave the signal to start the challenge. Iggy took only three steps and then turned to face the herd.

"When I stop up ahead, everyone stop. Don't run. Stay together, and the biggest ones in the group move to the outside. Protect the small ones on the inside. Got it?"

They all nodded. Iggy moved on and took a few more steps. The herd followed, more cautious and aware of Iggy's instructions. And then Iggy stopped.

He raised his nose to the sky and listened to the air move through the trees at the edge of the forest. He heard a branch snap behind them. Iggy whirled around and quickly moved to the back of the herd.

Two adult iguanodons crashed through the forest and advanced their targeted attack. At the last moment, Iggy ran forward and threw his body low against the ground. The adult iguanodons could not stop. They did not expect Iggy to charge them!

"Great work, Iggy! Keep going," his dad yelled proudly.

One of the adults tripped over Iggy's body. Iggy knocked the other down with a perfectly timed tail whip. He popped back up and turned to his practice herd. Iggy could only see dust surrounding the herd. They faced more attacks. The challenge continued.

"Over there!" Iggy's mom yelled. Iggy could not hear her. He focused on the battle.

Three other adult iguanodons came after the practice herd from the other side of the field. Iggy raced to the herd and saw something amazing! The bigger iguanodons in the practice herd defended from the outside. They protected the smaller ones. The adults could not break them apart.

By the time Iggy came to a stop between an adult and the edge of the herd, the challenge was completed. His plan had worked.

"Great job, Iggy!" Saber yelled. "You have won the challenge. You are ready to protect the herd with the adults."

Iggy had never felt better. He had won the hardest challenge for a young iguanodon. All of the iguanodons stomped their big back feet and hooted for him. His parents just stood back and watched proudly. No other iguanodon won the challenge that day or anytime soon.

Iggy walked home along the edge of the creek. The day's excitement began to fade. He started thinking about what winning the challenge really meant. *All of the herd will depend on* me. *I can't let them down. This is only the beginning.*

Guana and Dawn bounced after Iggy all the way back to the den. They were so excited that their big brother had become a new herd protector. Iggy was so deep in thought that he did not notice his sisters.

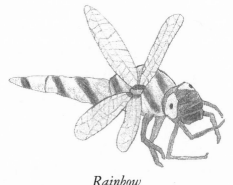

Rainbow

CHAPTER 5
Dragonflies

Back at the den, Iggy and his sisters found some shade and took an afternoon nap. They were very tired and slept hard. The midday sun burned off all of the heavy fog. The day grew hotter. Smoky haze still stood firm in the air.

Iggy heard a growl and sprang to his feet. Plant-Eater's Field was under attack from many t-rexes and raptors! They came out of the forest from all sides. Iggy looked all around and could not find his sisters or parents.

Raptors jumped on his back! He rolled to get them off and landed right under a t-rex. He raised his thumb spike but it was too late. The t-rex grabbed his arm in its mouth, between razor sharp teeth. Iggy growled, yelped, and tried to pull away from the monster.

"Be quiet!" Guana yelled. "We are trying to sleep. And stop pulling on my leg!"

Iggy shook his head side to side. He was dreaming. But it seemed so real. He stood up and looked around.

Iggy's mom and dad snacked on some untasty, dry grass nearby. A few young triceratopses played along the creek. Tall, scorched trees lost their remaining leaves to some hungry diplodocuses. Iggy took a deep breath. Everything seemed normal.

Juras saw that Iggy was awake and called to him. "Iggy, I have somewhere to take you. Come with me."

Iggy was not sure where they were headed. He did not normally go out with Juras by himself, except to eat. Still feeling a little sleepy, he trampled loudly out of the den to follow his father.

"We're just not going to get any more sleep today," Guana groaned.

"You aren't kiddin'," Dawn said slowly in the middle of a big yawn. "Let's go find something to do."

They had slept through the middle of the day. The sun was still high in the sky and hotter than normal.

"Let's go on top of Grassy Hill," Dawn said.

She started to run to the middle of Plant-Eater's Field. Guana followed, catching her right away. Dawn looked over at Guana as they trotted across the field and started up the hill. She smiled at Guana for just a second. Then, Dawn galloped away in the blink of an eye. Dirt and grass flew up in the air behind her.

"Hey, not so fast!" Guana yelled, laughing as she followed. She had to squint to keep the dust out of her eyes. Her younger sister was the fastest iguanodon in the field. No other plant-eater could catch Dawn when she wanted to run. Not even a diplodocus or a triceratops.

Guana reached the top of Grassy Hill. Her heart pounded fast. Dawn had already stopped breathing hard from the run. From Grassy Hill, they could see the rest of Plant-Eater's Field.

Most dinosaurs walked around the hill. It had a lot of tall grass and bushes that did not get eaten or trampled too much. It also had a lot of—

"Wow, look at all the dragonflies today!" Dawn yelled. "There must be one for every plant-eater in the field! I have never seen so many."

"Let's chase them," Guana said. "First to catch one wins."

The dragonflies came in all colors and sizes. The sisters gazed at large purple ones, little green ones, yellow-spotted ones, and everything in between.

Guana and Dawn hopped around and swung their heads side to side. They swiped with their arms and nibbled the air with their lips, careful not to use their teeth. The dragonflies flew faster, almost playfully, darting back and forth. They landed on the iguanodons' heads and backs just long enough to make them itch.

"We're never going to catch one of these," Guana called out.

Dawn didn't answer her. She had her eyes set on a big, slower dragonfly flitting just above her back. With her head turned over her shoulder, she crouched down. She kept her eyes focused on the dragonfly.

Wait, wait, a little longer, she said to herself. Dawn sprang up and bent her neck and head farther behind her. She moved as fast as a raptor. Turning halfway around in midflight, she nipped and grabbed the dragonfly by its wings, in between her lips.

"Got 'ya," Dawn mumbled since she couldn't move her lips.

Guana came over and looked at the dragonfly. It was beautiful.

"Look at those colors," Guana said in almost a whisper. "Blues, greens, reds, yellows. It has everything. Dawn, it looks like it really wants to get away. Please don't hurt it. Let it go now."

Dawn didn't want to hurt it, either. She carefully opened her lips. The dragonfly buzzed around her nose for a few seconds and then landed on her long snout. It just sat there and didn't move.

Every few seconds, the dragonfly fluttered its rainbow wings. It stayed on Dawn's nose. Guana came in real close and touched it with the tip of her moist nose. It still didn't move.

"Looks like you have a new friend, Dawn."

Dawn didn't talk. She barely breathed. She wondered how such a tiny animal could stay so close to her without being scared. This was a great day on Grassy Hill!

Mox the triceratops

CHAPTER 6
Mox and Jaz

Suddenly, the ground rumbled and shook on Grassy Hill. It bounced harder and harder. Something quickly approached! Guana and Dawn looked around just in time.

Jaz and Mox, two young triceratopses, thundered up the hill. They skidded to a stop, but not before they slammed into Guana and Dawn. The iguanodon sisters fell backwards and onto the ground.

"Jaz! What are you doing? Get away from me!" Dawn yelled as she stood up quickly. "We are playing here, and you are ruining it."

Guana slowly got off the ground. Dirt and grass covered her head and back. A clump of small flowers and bees sat and buzzed on her nose. She shook her head, and it all flew away.

"I don't like getting dirty, Mox, or being knocked on the ground," Guana said calmly. "We were here first, so you should go somewhere else."

"Ah, come on, Guana," Mox said. "We were just playing. Can't we stay up here, too? We are bigger than you. Maybe we will just play here if we want. Right, Jaz?"

Jaz thought for a moment and looked at Dawn and Guana. He was not sure. He also did not want to disagree with Mox.

"Sure, Mox, whatever you say," Jaz said.

Dawn was not happy at all. She suddenly realized that the dragonfly had fluttered away! Her eyes closed halfway and she crinkled her nose. Crouching on her hind legs, she looked at Jaz and then at Mox. She got ready for a fight.

"Uh, Mox, maybe we ought to go," Jaz said with a little tremble in his voice.

"Nah, I think I want to play … right … here," Mox said. He stomped his foot on a large patch of pretty red and purple flowers. Mox turned his head to look over Plant-Eater's Field.

Mox slowly announced, "It sure is a pretty day to spend up on a—"

Dawn moved so fast the ground didn't have time to rumble. She lowered her strong head and plowed into Mox's side. *Wham!* Dawn knocked Mox over so hard he rolled all the way over two times. He landed partway down the hill. Jaz could not keep from laughing. It was more of a snort, though.

Mox was surely not laughing. He raised his bruised body and lowered his three horns. Mox dug his front hoof through the grass. He then looked at Dawn. Dawn was ready for a fierce battle, too. She opened her long fingers and pointed her thumb spikes forward. She sat back, ready to pounce.

"Hey, guys, we don't have to play. But we don't have to fight either," Guana pleaded. "Let's all leave the hill."

Mox and Dawn took another step towards each other. They did not pay attention to Guana. The battle was about to begin.

All of a sudden, Dawn felt a little tickle on her back. She did not even have to look. Her mind cleared.

"Yeah, we can find something better to do," Dawn said. "Let's go."

Dawn and Guana walked away. Guana held her head high with pride that she had stopped a fight. She was good at that. Jaz and Mox just looked at each other a little confused. Then they chewed some grass.

Dawn turned her head over her shoulder and looked at her back. Blue, green, red, yellow. It was just as she had expected. The dragonfly fluttered and bounced. It landed a little closer to Dawn's head, where her body didn't move so much as she walked.

I will call him Rainbow, she thought to herself.

Iggy

CHAPTER 7
Far Forest

"Dad, where are we going?" Iggy asked.

"You'll see when we get there. Now stay close," his father said.

For a while, they walked along a path that Iggy knew well. It ran through the middle of the forest away from their den and Plant-Eater's Field. Iggy stayed right behind his father. The deep moaning sounds of the tall brachiosauruses faded behind them.

"Are we getting close?" Iggy asked every now and then. Juras did not answer for a while.

They reached the farthest point on the worn path that Iggy could remember. Around the next corner, the path suddenly stopped.

"What's here?" Iggy asked.

"Nothing," Juras said. "We will make our own way now. Come up next to me and stay closer."

The iguanodon son and father walked next to each other. They pushed sappy branches and small trees aside and stepped through tall bushes. The ground got bumpier and bumpier. It became harder to walk on due to the round, flat, and chipped rocks. The forest became thick for a while. Iggy then saw a clearing up ahead through the trees. He trotted faster.

"Iggy, *stop*!" his father yelled.

Iggy kept his feet still. The front half of his body poked through the trees. They stood on top of a high cliff just outside the forest. The clearing was just big enough for them to carefully walk onto. It was free from the trees and bushes and only a few feet from the edge of the drop off. Iggy looked all around and could not believe what he saw.

"Iggy, look down there," Juras said as he turned his head.

Iggy saw a massive dark green field far below them. It was surrounded by jagged cliffs on three sides. Waterfalls poured over some of the steep rock walls, making lakes and creeks throughout the grassland.

"Wow! Look at that!" Iggy yelled.

The cliff they stood on was much shorter than the others. It had a small path along the edge, which made its way down to the new field. The path ended at the lush floor of the new field.

"Look at all of those plant-eaters," Iggy said.

He saw large herds of brachiosaurus, triceratops, iguanodon, stegosaurus, and more. They roamed through the beautiful field. The far, open end of the field ended at a huge forest.

"This is just like our home, only bigger and greener," Iggy said.

Iggy noticed something else: the air smelled cleaner. No smoke.

"Dad, what is this place?" Iggy asked. "Why don't we live here? Everything about it seems better."

"Come with me and I'll show you," his father said.

They carefully walked along the path. Iggy and his father traveled lower and lower towards the new field. At the end, they were at the back of the field and the edge of the forest.

"This is Far Forest," Juras said. "Most of the meat-eaters, and the Evil T-Rex family, live in this forest. All of the plant-eaters in this field live in great danger every day."

"What are those?" Iggy asked. He looked at a massive pile of black and reddish rocks at the edge of the forest.

"Those are the fire rocks. They are left over from the Great Fire. The firewater burns our food and trees and makes the smoke. It used to be close to this forest. It left here a long time ago and left all of those rocks."

Iggy's father looked quickly down the edge of the forest. "Do you see that small stegosaurus over there next to the forest edge?" Juras asked. He turned his head to look a long way down the row of trees and bushes. Iggy then looked the same way.

"Yes, it looks to be only—"

In no time, the edge of Far Forest came alive! Three raptors came from the left and two t-rexes bolted from the right. The trees snapped and shattered. Meat-eaters pushed into the field with eyes set on their prey.

"No!" Iggy yelled. He trembled. Iggy dug his feet and thumb claws into the ground. He was not sure if he should run or help.

"Be very quiet," his father cautioned. "Stay hidden. We are far enough away to stay safe. We are too far away to help."

The t-rexes had longer to run. They did not want to cross over the fire rocks in front of them. The stegosaurus saw the raptors first and quickly turned to run the other way. A large t-rex circled around the fire rocks. It knocked the stegosaurus over with his tail, exposed his belly, and ... it was quick. It was over.

Iggy's stomach grumbled from disgust and anger. He thought of the stegosaurus herd back at Plant-Eater's Field.

"That is why we cannot live here, Iggy. It is too dangerous."

"But the air smells better here," Iggy noted.

"That's right," Juras said. "The firewater does not burn here now. But t-rexes are a bigger problem than the smoke we smell at home."

"Was that ... Evil T-Rex who caught the stegosaurus?" Iggy slowly asked. He shuddered to think how he would feel up close to Evil T-Rex. His belly twisted and he got dizzy.

"I'm not sure," his father said. "I only saw him once, a long time ago. But I will remember him if I see him up close again. I hope that never happens. Let's go before it gets too dark and before the meat-eaters see us."

Evil T-Rex

CHAPTER 8
Water Ground

Iggy and his father made their way back up the cliff. They passed the clearing at the top and entered the forest that would take them home. Juras chose a new path through the thick trees this time. They came to a different clearing. His father stopped before leaving the safety of the trees.

"Don't move," Juras said. "Something is not right." They both looked out into the clearing. Iggy didn't see anything. But he felt something moving. His feet tickled.

Iggy's stomach started churning again. He felt wobbly and wondered what his father knew that he did not. Iggy wanted to feel safe next to his father, but he was scared. He moved a little closer.

The ground moved slowly under their feet, and then faster. Iggy's heart raced, and he opened his eyes wider than ever before. And then, just like at Far Forest, the trees at the edge of the clearing erupted. Iggy's body tensed. This time, a herd of triceratopses ran into the clearing.

The three-horns galloped through the opening in the forest. Iggy let out his breath and felt better, but only for a second. A very large t-rex entered the clearing. He looked strong and very hungry. The tyrannosaurus was dark brown with deep, red eyes.

Iggy moved even closer to his father. He did not feel wobbly and he could not feel his stomach moving. He was completely numb and terrified! He stood frozen.

The t-rex had long and massive legs. It also had daggerlike toe claws and teeth. Huge jaws split open its large head. A deep, straight battle scar lined the left side of its face. Iggy wondered what one bite of the t-rex could do to him, or to his father. The only unusual item on the t-rex was the mostly useless tiny front arms. The beast really did not need them.

A second smaller t-rex ran out of the forest. They both chased the triceratopses and charged across the middle of the clearing to divide the herd. The large t-rex roared loudly. Iggy could see inside its enormous jaws. Iggy moved closer to Juras, slowly and quietly. The t-rex chose his prey, and with a final thundering step ...

Squish. Both t-rexes fell forward. The ground swallowed their lower bodies. All Iggy could see was the belly, head, and small front arms of each t-rex. The dirt moved all around them like thick, gooey water.

"Water ground!" Iggy said. "Did you ..."

"I have been through here before," his father replied. "I knew the water ground was there. But we still got very lucky today. Let's get home."

Iggy let out a deep breath. The danger seemed over but he was still scared. He kept his eyes glued to the t-rexes. Iggy and his father walked past the t-rexes along the edge of the clearing. Both meat-eaters bellowed, roared, and moved back and forth. They tried to get out of the slimy, sandy water ground. Every time they moved, they sank deeper and deeper.

Juras turned to make sure Iggy had followed him. Iggy had not. He stayed at the edge of the water ground, only a few steps from the t-rexes. The meat-eaters struggled and fought to stay alive. They were clearly trapped.

"Iggy! What are you doing?" his father yelled.

The smaller t-rex must be the son, Iggy thought. He looked into the forest and thought of his own family. He looked back at the t-rexes. Iggy crashed into the forest and pushed over a large tree. *Thump*. His father could not stop what happened next.

The tree landed across the water ground. Its large branches fell all around the t-rexes. The meat-eaters started to grab and pull themselves out of the trap. Bite by bite, they tried to escape the water ground.

"What have you done?" Juras exclaimed. "Do you see the scar on the big t-rex's face?"

Iggy did not answer. He just stood there and watched the two dinosaurs fight to stay alive. They quickly worked to pull themselves out. He could see their back legs now.

"I gave that t-rex the scar years ago," Juras added. "That is Evil T-Rex and his son! We have to get out of here!"

Iggy just stood there and watched. He was not sure why. His father would not leave his side. The t-rexes pulled themselves out of the water ground and stood looking over Juras and Iggy. Iggy could smell their stinky breath. The huge head of Evil T-Rex swayed back and forth. His wet teeth shined in the light. He let out a ferocious roar!

"I remember you, iguanodon!" Evil T-Rex yelled out. He looked at Juras. "You gave me this scar. I have never forgotten!"

Iggy wanted to hide behind his father. But for some reason he was not very scared now. He was not angry. He did not want to fight or run. He raised his eyes and looked straight ahead.

"And you," Evil T-Rex continued, "young iguan-odon. You are very brave. You are also very foolish.

I will make you my meal! But not today. Little T, let's go."

Little T and Iggy looked at each other square in the eye for a brief moment. Then the t-rexes ran back into the trees and back towards Far Forest. Iggy and his father stood alone in the clearing. They were shocked, and relieved, and confused.

"Iggy, I don't know why you did that," his father said. "We can talk when we get back to the den. We have to hurry before the sun falls. Let's go."

Iggy and his father ran back through the forest. They reached the narrow and curvy path that Iggy had used many times before. Iggy started to smell the smoky air as they approached Plant-Eater's Field. He thought of his den and the rest of his family. He kept running behind Juras. Iggy also thought of Far Forest and the better field. His mind then focused on Evil T-Rex and his son.

Why did I save the t-rexes? Why did they not attack us after they escaped the water ground? What is my dad going to say to me? What are the other plant-eaters going to say? What does this all mean?

Iggy remembered the herd challenge and his new
job protecting the plant-eaters. And then something
happened inside of him. He became less confused
the closer they got to home. Iggy stepped out into
Plant-Eater's Field behind Juras. He looked across
the creek and saw Dawn and Guana playing with a
dirty stump and a hoppy frog.

"Iggy, you're back!" Dawn yelled. She trotted
over to her brother.

He knew things would never be the same again.
Not for himself. Not for Guana, Dawn, or his parents. Not for Plant-Eater's field, his herd, or any of
the other plant-eaters. He would make sure of it. He
had a plan!

Iggy splashed across the creek and bounced into
his den.

CHAPTER 9
Iggy Needs Help

"Maya, Dawn, Guana, come here," Iggy's dad called. "I need to talk to all of you."

Dawn looked up. The stump and plugs of dirt hung from her mouth. Guana bumped the frog and it jumped next to the creek. They heard the commanding tone of their father's voice and quickly went to him.

"Iggy and I were at Far Forest." The girls and their mother gasped. "We saw Evil T-Rex and his son. We are—"

"Juras!" Maya yelled. "Why did you take Iggy over there? It is too dangerous! You have always told us that!"

"Mom, we are fine." Iggy said.

"I took Iggy there to show him what can happen if we are all not careful," Juras said. "He is a new protector of our herd. He needs to learn from the adults how to keep us safe. Iggy saw what can happen to dinosaurs that are not careful. Right, Iggy?"

Iggy remembered the terrible scene with the unfortunate stegosaurus. He started to answer his father.

"Right, but—"

"And Iggy saw the scar that I gave Evil T-Rex a long time ago when he tried to attack our herd," Juras continued. "We went too close to Far Forest many moons ago looking for food." Iggy's father looked down at the dry and dusty ground for a few seconds.

"All of the herd stayed together, and Evil T-Rex only took one of us," Juras added. "One loss in the herd is too many. We will stay safe here."

Juras turned to look directly at Iggy. "Iggy, Evil T-Tex knows you now. He will not be so forgiving if you meet again. I forbid you from leaving the safety of Plant-Eater's Field ever again. Do you understand this rule?"

Iggy did not want to disagree with his father, but he thought that there was a better way to stay safe. He wanted a better way for everything in their lives. He looked through the trees and could still see the murky sun sinking. Iggy looked back at

Juras, who awaited his answer. "Yes, Father," Iggy whispered. The parents moved to the edge of the den to talk.

"Guana, Dawn, get Jaz and Mox now and meet me at Grassy Hill," Iggy said.

"What! Those two snorty triceratopses?" Dawn said. "Mox is a bully and I don't like him."

"Everything will be fine, Dawn," Iggy said. "We have to put our differences aside and work together. Just trust me. I am a new herd protector, right?"

Guana decided to help Iggy convince Dawn. She figured he had something important for them.

"Hey, Dawn," Guana said. "Maybe your drag-onfly friend will be there. Let's go find him. We can get Jaz and Mox on the way and see what Iggy wants."

Dawn got a little twinkle in her eye thinking of Rainbow. She started trotting off, and Guana fol-lowed. Iggy saw Tail Whip practicing his special fighting moves in the grass. He walked out of the den to ask Tail Whip for help. Iggy's mother called out, "Iggy, where are you all going?"

"Just to find Dawn's dragonfly. We'll be back soon," Iggy answered. He walked away from his den and knew exactly what he had to do.

CHAPTER 10
Iggy's Plan

Iggy did not want to appear too excited, but he could not help it and started running fast, right at Tail Whip. *Smack!* Tail Whip got him square in the face.

"Ouch! Why did you whip me in head, Tail Whip?" Iggy asked.

"I thought you were a t-rex!"

"That's okay," Iggy said, rubbing his sore nose. "That was a good shot. Will you come with the others and me? We're having an important meeting."

Dawn, Guana, Jaz, and Mox stood on top of Grassy Hill as Iggy and Tail Whip arrived. Mox was still upset that Dawn had rolled him down the hill.

"Where's your little dragonfly friend, Dawn?" Mox said, poking fun at her.

Dawn did not answer. She just looked right at Mox and closed her eyes halfway. She then crinkled her nose and crouched back just like last time. Thinking more wisely this time, Mox backed away from the spunky little iguanodon.

"Everyone, settle down," Iggy said. "I have something to tell all of you. Today, I saw a better place to live. Smoke does not hang in the air. There is more fresh water and different plants and food to eat, just like there used to be here."

The others listened very closely to Iggy. This sounded great so far.

Iggy continued, "The field is far bigger than ours. Other plant-eaters live there, but it is big enough for all of us. It is next to Far Forest."

"Far Forest!" Mox and Jaz yelled at the same time.

"We are never supposed to go near there!" Mox said. "The adults forbid it."

"I was there with my dad today," Iggy said. "He took me there to show me how dangerous it is so that I will protect our herd here. But I know we cannot stay here any longer!"

Iggy paused and then said more calmly, "The firewater gets closer to here every day. We have less and less food and green field. There is everything we need at the new—"

"But, Iggy," Guana said patiently. "You heard Father. We are forbidden from leaving Plant-Eater's Field. It's too dangerous beyond here. We can't fight the t-rexes and other meat-eaters. There is nothing we can do about it."

"There *is* something we can do!" Iggy replied. "This is why I brought you here. The firewater left the edge of Far Forest a long time ago. It is a big pile of fire rocks now. We can use those rocks to protect the other field from the meat-eaters."

Guana started to think there might be something good about this plan. She continued to listen closely. They all became quiet and let Iggy continue.

Iggy added, "The field is already sealed on three sides by huge cliffs. We just need one more wall to make it a safe home. But it will take all of the adults, children, and herds from our field and the new field."

"It sure would take a lot of plant-eaters to make this happen!" Dawn said.

"If we work together, we can make it a safe place for all of us," Iggy said. "We will have better food, better air, and a bigger field. The other plant-eaters by Far Forest will get more protection."

"The food around here sure is getting pretty boring," Mox said.

"And the smoke gives me sniffle-snout," Tail Whip honked.

Dawn and Guana were also ready for a change. Dawn snuck a few peeks around Grassy Hill. She looked for Rainbow and felt a little sad that she may leave him. The young dinosaurs stood silently. The sun sank almost below the ground, and the night-time crickets started to chirp.

One by one, they turned their heads and looked into each other's eyes. They all started to smile, a crooked dinosaur smile. No one needed to say anything. They would all help with Iggy's plan.

"So how do we convince our parents and the other adults?" Jaz asked.

"I have an idea," Iggy replied. "Come on."

Tormon the brachiosaurus and council leader

CHAPTER 11
The Council of Elders

Iggy's parents left their den as usual for a regular meeting of the plant-eater elders. Their shadows from the sun almost disappeared. They could not miss any part of this important meeting.

"Come on, Maya. Keep up. We can't be late," Juras said.

The Council of Elders met every full moon after the last shadow from the sun. The oldest dinosaurs from all of the herds in Plant-Eater's Field gathered together. They always joined at the far end of the field. Juras and Maya were the oldest iguanodons in their herd, so they both went to the meetings.

Dinosaur shapes floated like ghosts from different sides and parts of the field onto a single path. They slowly walked down the center of the field as they had so many times before. Iggy's parents looked up at the moon.

"Look how bright the moon shines," Maya said. "The smoke is not so heavy tonight."

Iggy's father did not say anything. He just kept walking.

"Juras, what are you thinking? You are so quiet," she continued.

"I don't know," Juras said. "Something seems different tonight. I am not sure."

All of the dinosaurs gathered and took their places. Every herd had a leader that night: iguanodon, triceratops, stegosaurus, diplodocus, brachiosaurus, and all of the other plant-eaters from the field.

The eldest dinosaur stood above them all and demanded attention. He looked down, a long way down. Tormon was the largest of all the dinosaurs in Plant-Eater's Field. He was a massive brachiosaurus, over fifty thousand pounds and seventy feet long.

Tormon had a large hump on the top of his head and spiked ridges all the way down his long neck and back. He commanded respect. He had been the leader of their council for many years.

"Council of Elders, we come here again for the protection of our herds," Tormon said. "All leaders of the herds, speak in turn and tell us your thoughts."

Tormon lowered his snakelike neck. He settled his eyes first on the stegosaurus herd elder.

"My herd needs more room to find food," Grazor the stegosaurus declared. "We want to share land with the diplodocus and iguanodon herds."

"That's impossible," Doc said. "My diplodocus herd has too little space now. We can't share any more. We will defend our land if you try to take it."

"And the iguanodons have already had to go too far to find new greens," Juras added. "They will not accept anything worse."

It was quiet for just a moment. A few dinosaurs thought they heard something at the edge of the meeting grounds. They turned their heads, but then another leader spoke.

"There is no other solution. Each herd will have to take care of itself, and only the strongest will survive," Two Horn said. He was a very large triceratops. Two Horn had battled a t-rex a long time ago and lost his right horn.

None of the dinosaurs wanted to leave after Two Horn spoke. But no herd elder knew what else to say. It was so quiet, for so long, that even the crickets and bullfrogs stopped chirping and burping.

"And so it is decided," Tormon said. "We will find our own places in the field. *The strongest will survive.*"

No plant-eater wanted to accept that. But no one had any more ideas. It became silent.

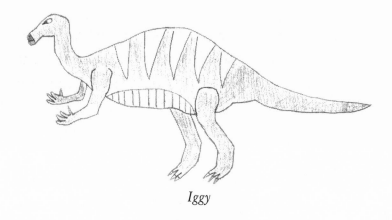

Iggy

CHAPTER 12
Iggy Steps In

"The strongest will lead their herd, all herds! We will all survive!" Iggy shouted as he entered the Council of Elders. Guana, Dawn, Mox, Jaz, and Tail Whip followed.

"What is the meaning of this?" Grazor bellowed.

"Young iguanodons have no place here," Doc added.

"They are my family, and their ... friends," Iggy's father said. "Iggy is a new herd protector, and we will listen to him."

Grazor snorted in protest, but no one disagreed with Juras. Iggy stepped into the middle of the council circle. He looked all around. His sisters and friends stood by his side. Iggy grumbled to clear his throat. He spoke with a deeper voice than ever before.

"My father took me to Far Forest and I saw what we *all* want: more food and fresh water, clear air, and enough room for all herds to live and grow."

Iggy then lowered his head and seemed to not know what else to say. All of the elders started to mumble. His father almost spoke, and then Iggy raised his eyes and continued more confidently.

"Far Forest is dangerous, too dangerous for us to live close by the way it is now. I am sure we all agree on that," Iggy said.

"Your father has always been right about that," Tormon said.

"But what if we had everything we wanted there: more food, fresh water, clean air, *and* protection? It would be better than what we have now. Our herds would not have to fight over land and food," Iggy added.

"You are brave but foolish," Doc said. "The meat-eaters are too powerful for us. We cannot join the field at Far Forest and survive."

All of the other elders agreed and mumbled back and forth. Dawn and Guana looked at Iggy. They felt defeated. Jaz and Mox snorted softly and looked embarrassed. Iggy turned his back to the council and took a step towards the forest. But he was still thinking and quickly turned back around.

"I was called brave and foolish not long ago," Iggy said. "By Evil T-Rex! I looked him in the eye and saw the scar my father gave him."

Iggy felt fearless. The elders paid more attention.

"He could have eaten my father and me near Far Forest, but he didn't," Iggy added. "I stood up to him. We both did."

Tormon lowered his head to listen more closely. The other plant-eaters did not make a sound.

"So if being brave and foolish means doing something important, I hope to be brave and foolish until the last full moon shines in my eyes! We need to take a chance and do something to help all plant-eaters." Iggy was almost out of breath.

The other elders now started to see that there was something special in this young iguanodon. They stopped muttering and snorting. Tormon and the others stopped wondering why this new herd protector was there that night. They listened closely.

"You speak as though you have a plan, son of Juras," Tormon said.

Iggy proceeded to tell them all about his plan. He described the three cliffs, the perfect grass, air, and water at the field by Far Forest. He explained how they could use the fire rocks to make a wall of protection against the meat-eaters.

Juras and Maya gave each other a quick smile. The other elders looked at them and wondered how they had raised such a smart, young leader.

"How can we make such a wall of rock, and how can we make this whole plan happen?" Grazor asked.

"It will take all of us," Iggy said. "Young and old dinosaurs from our herds and the other herds by Far Forest. We have to send a group to the other field and talk to the plant-eaters who live there."

Iggy continued, "We have to explain that we all have the same needs: a safe place to live and enough food for everyone."

All of the elders nodded their old and bumpy heads. They at least felt safe at Plant-Eater's Field, but the food was getting harder and harder to find.

"The other field has better food and grasslands, but the meat-eaters can easily attack the plant-eaters," Iggy added. "We can all live together at the new field with the right protection, but it will take all of us to make it happen. We can only survive together."

Iggy then looked up at Tormon. "Will you go to the field by Far Forest and talk to the other plant-eaters?" Iggy asked.

Tormon thought for a moment. He had been the council leader for a long time. He had also seen no other dinosaur in Plant-Eater's Field before Iggy care so much about all of the dinosaurs from all herds. No other dinosaur had given them so much hope.

"Plant-Eater's Field will send a group of dino-saurs to the other field," Tormon commanded. "That group will discuss this new plan with the leaders of the other field. We will have a vote to decide who will lead our group."

Iggy was happy and started to walk away with his sisters and friends.

"Great job, Iggy," Dawn said.

"Yeah, they sure listened to you," Guana added.

Mox and Jaz pointed their horns in the air as they all started to leave the council. They were proud.

"I propose that the leader of this group is ... *Iggy!*" Tormon declared.

Was it quiet, loud, or somewhere in between? Iggy could not recall. There was a quick vote and no one disagreed with Tormon. The Council of Elders at Plant-Eater's Field erupted in bellows, hoots, thumps, and bumps. Everyone was hopeful and happy. All of the other dinosaurs in the field wondered what had happened. They waited for the elders to return and give the news, the new hope. They would all hear about Iggy's plan.

Iggy did not remember going home that night. He did not remember all of the other dinosaurs who followed him and his family back to their den. He could only recall lying down next to Guana and Dawn as he always had. Iggy fell asleep soundly with clearer thoughts than he had in weeks.

CHAPTER 13
Families and Leaders

A screeching bird woke Iggy up the next morning. He stood up and stretched. It was still early, and it was especially foggy. He looked around and could barely see to the creek.

"Hey, where are you?" Iggy called out to his family. No one heard him.

Guana, Dawn, and his parents savored a morning bath. His mother rolled on her back in the creek and wiggled her legs back and forth. Dawn tapped her front foot lightly into the running water. It was just enough for small splashes to bounce straight up onto her nose and chin. She liked that.

Dawn had not slept well. She was nervous about leaving Rainbow behind. There was nothing she could do. At least the water was cool that morning and felt good.

"Hey, where are you!" Iggy called out louder this time.

Guana was knee deep in the creek water and peered at a spotted fish swimming aimlessly around her. Every now and then, the fish popped to the surface and ate a water bug. She heard Iggy this time.

"Iggy's awake," Guana called out after turning to look towards the den.

Juras left the edge of the creek and came over to Iggy. The rest of the family followed.

"I am very proud of you," he said to Iggy. "You have given us new hope with your plan. But there is hard work ahead for us all. It could be very difficult. We could lose some of the herd making such a big change."

Iggy looked through the fog. The rest of Plant-Eater's Field started to wake up. He saw Tormon's head above the heavy white mist, and he heard a triceratops snort and gallop nearby. His plan was great. Iggy also realized that everyone would depend on him and his ideas to save the herd. He was nervous but did not want anyone to see that. He did not answer his father. Juras could see Iggy's doubt.

"Come with me," Juras said. "I need to take you somewhere you have not been in a long time."

Iggy's dad turned slowly and trotted out of the den. Iggy quickly moved to his father's side. They ran through the heavy fog. Small, cool water droplets bounced on their faces, and the fog swirled behind them. Iggy and Juras headed to the other side of Grassy Hill. His father stopped at a large mound of dirt, sticks, branches, and stones by the edge of the wet field.

"Iggy, do you remember this place?"

"This is where Popodon closed his eyes and never woke up," Iggy replied.

"That's right, Iggy. Your grandfather was a great dinosaur and a true leader. He brought us all to Plant-Eater's Field a long time ago, before you were born," his father said.

Juras continued, "He became very old. When he died, the other dinosaurs from all herds came to his side and thanked him one last time. I wish you could have met him."

"I remember your stories about Popodon. Those were my favorite when I was younger," Iggy said.

"Plant-Eater's Field looked back then just like the field by Far Forest does now," his father said. "Better

food, more land, fresher water. It was more dangerous when Popodon first brought us here. Then the
meat-eaters moved to Far Forest."

Iggy wanted to give his family and the others
a better life. But he knew there could be problems
ahead if they left Plant-Eater's Field.

"It is easier to settle for what we have now,"
Juras said. "It is easier not to change and not to take
risks."

Iggy agreed. At the same time, he knew something had to change.

"But the easy way is not always the best," Iggy's
dad said. "You will be taking us all down a path
that Popodon showed us a long time ago. Are you
sure you are ready for such a difficult task?"

Iggy paused and then looked at his father. He
knew he had a great plan.

"I know we will be doing the right thing," Iggy
said. "It is scary, but I am confident and I will be
strong for all of our herds."

They did not need to say anything more. Iggy
knew why his father brought him to Popodon's rest-
ing place. He no longer had any doubts. He was not

nervous anymore. Iggy ran ahead of Juras this time, back to the den. He felt strong. Something was different around the den when he arrived.

The fog slowly lifted. Iggy could see many new shadows around their home. All of the dinosaurs from the Council of Elders stood there with their families. Other dinosaur families had also joined them.

"Iggy," Tormon said. "Everyone knows of your plan now. We are ready to send a group to the field by Far Forest. Who do you want to go with you?"

This was the first time the entire herd looked at Iggy for an answer. This was the moment when he became their leader. He looked around and called out names.

"Dad, Guana, Dawn, Mox, Jaz, Tail Whip, Saber, Doc, and Grazor. We will leave soon. Have a long drink from the creek. Let's all get ready."

The herd looked for a new beginning from the young iguanodon leader.

CHAPTER 14
The Distant Herds Meet

The group of young and older dinosaurs traveled down the long path through the forest. They all wondered how the other plant-eaters would accept them. Finally, they emerged from the forest and into the clearing. The new field stretched out below them. Lush, green trees blew in the clear breeze.

"It really is beautiful, Iggy!" Dawn said.

"I could sure live there!" Guana added.

"Down there," Iggy called out. "That is where we are going. We will follow the edge of this cliff to the field. Stay close to the fire rocks and away from the edge of Far Forest when we get down there."

They traveled carefully in line along the cliff. Iggy led the group. The plant-eaters in the field quickly spotted the newcomers far up on the cliff. Iggy and his group could hear the defensive moans and grumbles erupting throughout the field below. He watched as the brachiosaurus and stegosaurus herds quickly huddled together. The other dinosaurs approached the edge of the field where Iggy's group would enter. *They are just like us*, thought Iggy. *They work together.*

Iggy's group emerged onto the field at the bottom of the cliff. They walked near the fire rocks. Iggy turned to look closer at the jagged and irregular rocks. Some of the rocks were small, some large. *There will be enough rocks for a great wall if all of the dinosaurs help*, he thought.

Iggy led his group down the middle of the field to meet the other herd leaders who had gathered. The other leaders clearly did not welcome the arrival of the newcomers. The new herd stood defensively, with stiff tails, raised backs, and menacing looks on their faces. Iggy had come too far to be intimidated. He lowered his head to show his submission to the other dinosaurs. But his voice was clear and strong: "My name is Iggy.

"Our herds live over the cliffs at Plant-Eater's Field," he continued. "We are running out of food and space. We need a better place to live. We have a plan that will help us and help you."

"This is our land," a large stegosaurus quickly retorted. "We fight hard every day to keep it and do not want to share." He sniffed and scratched at the ground and shook his small head.

"You have much more than you need here," Iggy said, trying to convince them. "There is enough room for all of us. Please listen to my—" His voice began to quiver.

"Your group sends a young iguanodon here to tell us to give you our land and food!" snorted a triceratops.

The rest of the plant-eaters from the new field bellowed and laughed. They did not take Iggy seriously. They did not see him as a leader.

Iggy thought. He then asked, "How many of you have lost someone in your family or a friend to the meat-eaters in Far Forest? How long can you live this way before there will not be enough of you to survive?"

That quieted down the group. Iggy continued.

"Our field was once dangerous, too, but now it is not. We know what it is like to live and not worry about the meat-eaters every day. But we have other problems."

The plant-eaters from both herds all thought about their struggles. They all wished things would be better.

"What if we could solve all of our problems together?" Iggy asked.

They all heard the distant and fierce roar of a t-rex from deep within Far Forest. Stomp, an older brachiosaurus from the new field, slowly walked towards Iggy.

"Tell us about your plan, young iguanodon," Stomp asked.

Stomp the brachiosaurus

CHAPTER 15
Herds Unite and Battle

Iggy knew it was time to convince the other herd. He had this one chance.

"Your field is protected by three cliffs," Iggy said. "One side opens to Far Forest. We can all work together and build a wall along this edge to protect us from the meat-eaters."

The new plant-eaters listened closely but were not convinced yet. How could they accomplish this?

Iggy continued, "We will create a new home for all plant-eaters who need a new safe place to live."

"How will we build this wall?" Stomp asked.

"Follow me," Iggy replied.

Iggy walked towards the fire rocks, and they all followed. He noticed again how good the air smelled at this new field. The grass was so green and lush everywhere. In the distance, he heard the smattering sounds of water falling from the cliffs into lakes and streams.

They got closer to the fire rocks and he heard a familiar sound, an awful one! Low, deep rumbles oozed out of Far Forest, this time much closer. There seemed to be more shapes and shadows in the trees than what Iggy recalled a short time before. They could not waste any time!

"He has taken us too close to Far Forest!" a triceratops screamed. "Everyone, scatter!"

"No!" Iggy directed. They were already very close to the fire rocks. "Large dinosaurs get on the outside! Smaller ones stay next to the fire rocks! If you run, you will be taken!"

All of the dinosaurs listened to Iggy, and they did so just in time. The t-rexes came out of Far Forest, growling and snarling. They pounded the ground with their clawed feet and ran right at the group of plant-eaters. Their white teeth shined. The smaller dinosaurs, including Guana and Dawn, huddled against the fire rocks. The larger plant-eaters stood between them and the t-rexes.

"Doc, look out!" Iggy yelled.

Doc turned and whipped his snakelike tail just in time. He sent a large t-rex tumbling backwards, knocking down two other meat-eaters. The other large plant-eaters worked hard to protect the herd.

Long necks rose up and stomped down with their powerful legs. Stegosauruses swung their spiked tails and connected just enough to keep the t-rexes away. Iggy's father sliced his thumb spikes side to side. The larger triceratopses stood shoulder to shoulder and charged at the meat-eaters if they came too close.

Two t-rexes went behind the rocks and looked right at the younger dinosaurs. The hungry meat-eaters would not cross over the fire rocks. And then it happened. All of the t-rexes went back into Far Forest.

"We have never defeated them, until now!" said a diplodocus.

"They will not stay away long," Juras said. "We need to go."

Stomp felt a new sense of hope along with all of the other plant-eaters at the field. He lowered his head and looked down at Iggy.

"How can we build this wall?" he asked.

Iggy looked down at the fire rocks. They stood directly on top of the solution.

"The meat-eaters will not walk over these," Iggy said. "I saw them go around them the other day when we came here. And we saw it again just now."

The plant-eaters all looked at the rocks. They wondered if their solution could be so simple.

"If all of our herds cooperate, we can push the fire rocks high along the edge of the field by Far Forest," Iggy said. "We will be safe. But we all have to help. We will go back and bring the rest of our herds."

The plant-eaters from the new field all agreed with Iggy's plan. They walked away from Far Forest and back to the safer middle grasslands. Juras, Grazor, Mox, Jaz, and the others started back to Plant-Eater's Field. Iggy, Guana, and Dawn stayed for a minute and looked at the beautiful fire rocks. They wondered if there would really be enough. They talked about a new home.

Little T

CHAPTER 16
A Favor Returned

Iggy, Guana, and Dawn needed to leave the fire rocks. The rest of their group was too far away up the cliff. They had to catch up, but they saw something that kept them there longer.

"What's that?" Dawn asked. She moved beyond the far side of the fire rocks and inched closer to a steep drop off. She gazed at other fields far below them.

"Look at those herds: more plant-eaters!" Guana said. "We have to tell them to join us."

"Those are not plant-eaters," Iggy said. "Look at how they run. They are traveling in packs and chasing something in the tall grass. Those are raptors!"

The three iguanodons stood above the drop off. Dawn was too close to the edge, and too far from Iggy for him to help. The ground gave way under her! Dawn kicked and tried to move backwards. More dirt and rocks tumbled under her desperate feet. She started to go over the side. In a flash, it got worse!

Little T had stalked them from within Far Forest. He was in the last t-rex attack and never lost sight of them. For a smaller t-rex, he was still much larger than Dawn. He was close to her.

Flop! Little T landed on his belly at the edge of the drop-off. He grabbed Dawn's back leg in his mouth just before she fell away from him. Dawn squealed in pain and surprise. With his powerful back legs and sharp claws, Little T pulled his prey back away from the edge and stood up. He held her off the ground as she wriggled and screamed.

Iggy and Guana ran at Little T, not sure what they would do when they got there. Iggy skidded to a stop. Guana stood at his side in front of Little T.

Plop! Dawn landed on the ground hard. She desperately rolled and kicked away from the young t-rex. Little T had let her go! She quickly moved behind Iggy. Iggy looked at Little T and then back at Dawn to make sure she was okay. She seemed unharmed but very scared.

"I remember you, iguanodon," Little T growled. "Back in the clearing, you saved me and my father." With a clearer voice, Little T said, "Thank you." Little T and Iggy just stared at each other. Iggy stayed quiet.

Iggy's father turned around from high on the cliff. He saw Dawn and Guana still at the fire rocks with Iggy and Little T. Hidden within Far Forest, Evil T-Rex also watched his son and the others.

Iggy took a step closer to Little T and sniffed at him. He turned his body to the side and looked away. Iggy had a new sense about this t-rex.

"Iggy. What's happening?" Dawn called out. She was scared and confused. Iggy did not answer her. He stayed quiet.

Little T took a step closer to Iggy and growled. It was not a mean growl, though. It was more like the rumble you hear when two t-rexes meet each other. Then, Little T scampered away in a flash. Dust and rocks flew in the air as he ran back into Far Forest. By that time, every plant-eater from the cliff and from the new field watched. They all saw what had happened.

"Who knew my big brother was so brave!" Dawn exclaimed.

"Iggy, you are one lucky iguanodon," Guana added.

Iggy did not feel lucky or brave. He wondered about how Little T had acted. *Maybe even the t-rexes are not so different*, he thought. Iggy saw bigger changes ahead for the plant-eaters and meat-eaters beyond his plan and beyond the wall. The three iguanodon siblings ran along the side of the cliff and joined the rest of their group. Juras smiled and let Iggy take the lead.

Guana

CHAPTER 17
A New Home

Iggy could not stop thinking about how Little T had saved his sister. Dawn was still in shock. Guana thought she knew all about meat-eaters. She was not so sure now.

"What happened back there?" Dawn asked Iggy. She was right behind him on the path through the forest.

Dawn was still wobbly and confused after hanging from a t-rex mouth. She bumped into a tree on the side of the path every now and then. Iggy told her how Little T had watched them from Far

Forest. Guana added how Little T jumped to grab her, landing on his belly and clawing the ground with his back feet.

"*Wow!* I would have been a raptor dinner if I went over the cliff," Dawn said.

"I was scared, really scared," Guana yelled ahead. She was right behind Dawn.

They reached the edge of the forest near Plant-Eater's Field and crossed the creek. Most of the other plant-eaters waited for them at Iggy's den. They all stood quietly. The larger plant-eaters shifted their weight from foot to foot, either because they were nervous or just really heavy or both.

Iggy, Guana, Dawn, his father and the other dinosaurs in their group reached the den. Iggy looked at all of the other plant-eaters. He saw the sparkle of hope in their weary eyes. Iggy looked at the rocks that he slept by since he was a baby. He listened to the creek rippling by the den. Juras give him a nod.

"*We have a new home!*" Iggy announced.

Plant-Eater's Field boomed with the happy hoots and hollers from every dinosaur! A new energy flowed through the herds. They ran and played. Plant-eaters laughed and talked about having better land, food, and a place to raise their families.

"We will leave tomorrow morning," Iggy added. "Get good sleep and a full meal. We will have a lot of work to do."

The herds drifted into the darkness at Plant-Eater's Field for the last time. Everyone made sure they grazed longer that night. Dawn and Guana even chewed all of the pretty flowers they loved to watch grow on Grassy Hill. Dawn left a couple flowers in case Rainbow was still around. Mox was with her, and he made sure not to step on them. Dawn noticed Mox's extra attention to the last flowers. *Maybe Mox isn't that bad after all*, Dawn thought to herself.

"Thanks, Mox," Dawn said.

Mox pretended not to hear her, but he was happy that Dawn noticed. *Maybe Dawn is not so bad*, he thought.

They didn't have to worry about leaving food at Plant-Eater's Field for the next day. They all went to sleep with full bellies and warm thoughts of their new home.

Iggy had trouble staying asleep and tossed and turned all night. He thought of their new challenges and what kind of den his family would have at the new field. Guana and Dawn were so tired from the day's events, they didn't notice Iggy's restlessness. They fell asleep quickly.

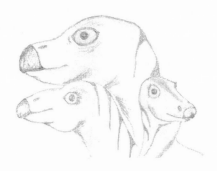

CHAPTER 18
Fire Rock Field

Iggy awoke the next morning when he felt the ground rumble. Every dinosaur from every herd in Plant-Eater's Field walked together towards Iggy's den.

"Guana, Dawn, Iggy, come get some water before we leave," Iggy's mother called. His father already stood at the creek with her.

One last time, Iggy, his sisters, and his parents stepped into the creek together and drank. Iggy was going to miss his home. As Iggy took a last sip, he could also taste the smoke in the air. The firewa-

ter approached even closer to Plant-Eater's Field.
As long as he had his family, he figured he could
make any place his home.

All of the plant-eaters were ready to go. They
started on the path through the forest and left Plant-
Eater's Field. The walk seemed very long to the
excited dinosaurs. Iggy carefully led them through
the trees and bushes once they traveled off of the
main path. They reached the cliffs and worked their
way down towards the field.

One by one, each dinosaur caught a first glimpse
of their new home and paused long enough to get
bumped from behind. Once a long line of plant-
eaters starts moving, it cannot easily stop. After a
while, they reached the field. They walked to the
middle to meet the other plant-eaters. Stomp came
over to Iggy and his father.

"Did all of your herds get here safely, Iggy?"
Stomp asked.

Iggy looked around behind him. He saw the signal from Tail Whip at the back of the group. Every
dinosaur had arrived safely.

"Sure did," Iggy said. "Are you ready to get to work?"

With that, all of the plant-eaters joined together and made their way to the fire rocks. Iggy picked a large rock and climbed up on it. He looked out over the massive number of large and small plant-eaters.

"We need half of the largest plant-eaters to line up between the rocks and Far Forest," he said. "The rest of us will move the rocks into place. If you get tired, switch with one of the guards by Far Forest."

The large herd started to move. Iggy was not done with his instructions.

"If meat-eaters come, don't run. Stay together and protect the smaller ones," Iggy added.

Iggy's parents moved the first stones. Diplodocus and brachiosaurus herds lined up to protect the rest. Some of the larger stegosauruses also stood with the long necks. Iggy watched from the side for a few minutes.

"It's a pretty sight," Iggy heard. He turned to his right and saw another iguanodon standing close. He focused his eyes on a girl about his age. Iggy did not know her from Plant-Eater's Field. She had been living in the new field already.

"My name is Mag," she said. "You must be Iggy. I have heard about you." She smiled really big.

Iggy blushed. He didn't know what to say. He opened his mouth and ... burped! *Did I really do that?* He was so embarrassed!

"You sure are a cute one," Mag said. She giggled and trotted towards the fire rocks. Turning back for a second, she looked at Iggy.

"Come find me later and I'll show you a great place for your den!" she yelled.

Iggy smiled. He liked this place even more.

The fire rock wall went up quicker than Iggy had expected. It still took most of the night. So many dinosaurs pushed, pulled, kicked, and rolled rocks everywhere. Mox and Jaz got pretty good at grabbing rocks in between their horns. They tossed them high into the air, on top of the wall.

"Great toss!" Jaz yelled. Mox had thrown a larger rock higher up on wall with perfect aim.

The rest of the triceratops herd bulldozed the rocks with their heads and necks into large piles at the bottom of the wall. They moved the rocks into place all the way down the edge of Far Forest. Guana and Tail Whip moved smaller rocks around at the bottom of the wall. They focused on plugging holes and gaps.

"Hey, Guana, look at this," Tail Whip said. With a swipe of his tail, he swatted a pile of small rocks against the wall into some remaining holes.

"You sure are good with that tail!" Guana said. She smiled and knew how proud Tail Whip was of his special tool and weapon.

Dawn also worked with the smaller rocks but with less energy than her sister. She still missed her colorful friend. *It is so silly to worry so much about a little dragonfly*, she thought. She continued to fill holes.

"This is coming along great!" Iggy yelled out to the large herd. "We are almost done. Keep up the good work!"

The plant-eaters gladly worked hard for Iggy and their new plan. Just before morning, they finished the wall. All of the dinosaurs moved to the field side of the wall and placed the last rocks. At no time during the night did the meat-eaters attack or even make any noise. They quietly watched from deeper within Far Forest. Their world changed overnight, and they could only wonder how it would continue to change.

"Wow!" Guana said to Iggy. "This is great!"

The new herd stepped away from the wall to admire their work. It ran from one end of Far Forest to the other and connected the cliffs at the ends of the field. It also sealed off the path that they had traveled down. The wall was taller than the back of the largest brachiosaurus and as thick as three triceratopses. Meat-eaters could not come through it or over it. Juras and Maya stood with their son.

"You should be proud of yourself, Iggy," his father said.

"And you have saved so many dinosaurs," Iggy's mother added.

"I am proud of all the herds," Iggy said. "We all took a chance and ended up better. We all believed in something and worked hard to make it happen."

The herds from two distant fields mixed and spread through Iggy's new home. Dawn and Guana ran at Iggy from his left and his right. He pretended not to notice. *Slam!* All three rolled and kicked.

"Hey, big brother, what do we do now?" Guana asked playfully. She nipped at his neck, and he threw her off to the side.

"Can we go exploring?" Dawn asked.

Suddenly, she felt the tickle again on her back. She quickly looked behind her. Rainbow seemed even brighter and more colorful at their new home! *This place is perfect now*, Dawn thought.

"This is our new home. Let's go meet the new dinosaurs, and yes, you should go exploring," Iggy replied.

Dawn ran off faster than ever before. Rainbow decided to fly next to her this time.

"Show off!" Guana yelled after her. "You better not slow down. I am right behind you!" Guana trotted away. Mox, Jaz, and Tail Whip ran after them, and they all charged down the field.

Iggy turned and looked at his parents again. They stood together, rubbed necks, and then walked through the fresh, wet grass. He knew they were happy. Iggy then turned his back to the new wall.

The sun rose behind him over Far Forest. He could not be happier.

Rays of light shined through the non-smoky air and danced over the top of the new wall. Iggy squinted his eyes as the light slowly made its way down to his new home, down Fire Rock Field. This was Iggy's first sunrise over Fire Rock Field. It was the first of many.

His mind spun faster and faster. There was still so much to figure out. *Will all of the new dinosaurs accept us? Where will my family make our den? Is there any other way for the meat-eaters to get into Fire Rock Field? What other adventures or dangers await us? Can I be a successful leader in the future?*

Iggy was tired. He did not want to think about those things for a while. He looked at a large lake further down Fire Rock Field. It caught falling water from the cliffs. Sunshine slowly made its way along the shore and glistened in the water. Mag stood by herself next to the lake. The sun just started to show her pretty brown and tan colors. *Maybe I need to get to know this iguanodon better*, Iggy thought.

Mag had seen Iggy when he was talking to his parents. She turned away for a while. She looked back again to find Iggy standing next to her. He was home.

ABOUT THE AUTHOR

John Dolbey lives in the Midwest with his wife and daughter. He began feeding his daughter's deep fascination of dinosaurs with countless bedtime and drive-to-school adventure stories. The creation of Iggy, Guana, and Dawn is the result of years of collaborative character building. John's first book, *Sunrise Over Fire Rock Field*, is a tribute to his daughter, her love of dinosaurs, and those adventurous iguanodon siblings. John and his daughter are still telling stories and coming up with new journeys for Iggy and his sisters.